Other Times, Distant Lands

By Lee Garratt

ISBN: 978-1-989940-01-3

Dimensionfold Publishing

dimensionfold.com

Contents

The road goes ever on and on

A boy,
I opened the book
and read
"In a hole in the ground there lived a hobbit"
and a world slowly unfurled to me
of forests and mountains and dragons,
of pipes and tales and elves,
of songs and caves and goblins,
and I have never really left.

My father,
whose book it was,
must also have dwelled in these lands,
thought of them, whilst negotiating an M62 exit,
thrilled to slowly leave the Shire
with each step closer to the unknown,
danger on the other side of the Brandywine,
a vast wilderness mapped more by story than charter,
where glittering dwarven chambers were rumour
and beasts unreckoned with delved in the dark,
to turn aside from this,
back to his accounts,
shipping logs,

tax duties.

My son finished the same book yesterday
red leather, gold embossed, rubbed away by use,
ran in to tell me, breathless, of Bard slaying Smaug.
I watched him read
tried to walk with him through Mirkwood
but I couldn't follow him
you never can
not really.

I look up from the book
and my son has moved away now,
spell broken,
chattering of this and that.
'what's for lunch'.

I remember my father
late at night at the dinner table
hunched over the Silmarillion.
What was it he read there?
Where did he wander?

Fake News

Even from the destruction wrought in the colonisation event, the mass of texts we amassed from the Earthlings was incredible. Beyond count. Physical texts of all kind. Whole buildings full of them ('libraries'). We were astonished. We are a very different society. Our recordings were scant. Never private. Always public. Always purposeful. That a few of us, tasked to the immense, impossible task of sieving the earth for things of use, have been influenced there is no doubt. One cannot not, so rich is the brew. Texts of their account of our colonisation are always of interest, being so different in perspective to ours. I was young then. Frightened. The following was recovered from a computer found on the islands referred to as Britain.

We were all so excited. That's what I remember. We still didn't have a television, not unusual in 1968, so my father announced one night that we would go to the pub. The whole village was there, watching on the television. Much of what I remember is incidental. The noise, the smoke. But a stillness settled in the final moments and we all watched those first steps. I was held high at the back of the pub and watched them bounce effortlessly across the surface.

After the.... what I saw, the atmosphere changed of course. Confusion. Shouts. Cries. We were hurried home. Next day no one spoke of it. My parents never did to my knowledge. In the immediate aftermath, a decision was taken by panicked TV executives to immediately get rid of the transmission. No copies were ever made.

It was different for us kids though. Games of moon monster proliferated (like tag really) but quickly banned. It became an obsession I suppose for all of us for a time. Magazines and comics abounded in wild speculation.

Like everything though, after a while, the whole *event* started to fade. Subsequent surveys from earth never showed anything despite the best efforts of the unprecedent Soviet/US cooperation. Neither did the later, militarised, Gemini landings. Nothing.

Generally, the topic was becoming passé I suppose. I was one of the last to be able to enrol on the specialist Moon degree at university; they all came to an end a short time later.

The 'event' continued to pop up from time to time. I suppose by the 1980s though, I noticed there had been somewhat of a shift in how it was reported. More often than not, it was in the kind of shows where it was placed alongside Big Foot and the Loch Ness monster. And then the first rumours that it was all faked. When I first came across this in the early 90s it was laughable. At least I thought so. Amongst younger people this cynicism was much more prevalent.

The dawn of the internet fuelled all this of course. Conspiracy theorists brought the whole subject back into vogue for a while. Of course, when the American President (who had actually watched it live as I had done) referred to it jokingly, alongside the BBCs coverage of him, as 'fake news' that's when it went viral. It became something of a touchstone somehow. If you believed in the 'moon monster' you were somehow suspect.

2019 was when things got nasty. In a lecture a group of students stood up and started shouting at me. And then, quite quickly I noticed I became side-lined. Moved on to an obscure literature course. I took early retirement then.

So what did I see? It's strange now. So vivid yet so unclear. I saw a grey shape emerge from the shadows. The astronauts hadn't seen it yet. Slow and cumbersome it seemed. Organic like a tree almost. Then it rushed with incredible speed and fluidity, like mercury. Just ripped them apart.

My own family has also been affected. It caused an argument around the table one Christmas. My husband had passed and I was on my own. I suppose it is normal for the elderly to become diminished in some ways but to have your children laugh and mimic you....

They still loved me of course. I am old now. It was nice of them to bring me out of the home last week for my birthday. A lunar eclipse of the sun. When the first flare went off we all looked at it. Then another. Then hundreds peppering the surface. That was five days ago. They all landed in China. Not one was destroyed by the entire combined military might of our planet. Not one. At this moment the picture is confused. It's funny but, after being derided for so long, people now clamour for my attention. I don't have much of relevance to say in all truth. I was an arts professor really, specialising in the cultural impact of the landings.

I don't tell them all of what I remember though. (Why this is I am not entirely sure). How Buzz froze. How his stillness seemed to fool them. I did see that. I don't know why I don't tell anybody. I'm old. I'm sure they must have worked that out already in Asia but it doesn't seem to have stalled them much. Maybe I just want to see them. And they get closer every hour.

We were lucky. That is widely accepted now. That the earthlings surpassed us in every measure except one is undeniable (though some do). Our knowledge of what they refer to as relativity though was superior. A simple grasping of the main point that gave us our cloaking, our camouflage. Our soldiers could not be hit for we could not be seen if we could manipulate light. It was an unfair fight. A slaughter. It took a while but every earthling has been killed. And their records, innumerable, are what we are left with. All I can do is read and bear witness.

Outbreak

It was on a wet October day in 2017 that an 8-year-old boy, whilst walking to his school in his Northamptonshire village, said the following sentence, "What are we going to *dilal* tonight Daddy". When his father queried him, this was changed to "*dilal* Daddy?! What are we going to do?"

Of course, such childish nonsense language, was and is totally natural, but what struck the father odd at the time was the child's reaction to his initial questioning; a benign indifference to his increasing bemusement. The father remembers that this minor scene only came to an end when they reached the school gates. Upon picking him up at the end of the day, he brought the subject up again, but being met by seeming incomprehension, put it as aside as one of those odd childish mysteries that sometimes occur and didn't give it much thought until several weeks later.

Investigations have since revealed that over the weeks that followed, *dilal* became a common word in the Braunston playground and then slowly crept out into the surrounding villages and towns. This was followed by other 'words' such a *gurab, kai, ming* amongst others.

The couple of teaching staff survivors that remain, remember that this behaviour was initially a source of amusement amongst the staff and, even, was thought of in a positive light; a humorous anecdote demonstrating the boundless imagination and playfulness of the child. There was even an appointment with the local newspaper to come and talk to the children about this new playground language.

The circumstances why this appointment was cancelled are not clear, but it appears that teachers became frustrated by the seeming indifference[1] amongst the children (for it was nearly all of them now) about the impending visit of the newspaper. When the actual topic of the visit was brought up, the children remained stoically apart. Not rude or confrontational but a total avoidance of the topic. The teachers' increasingly heated inquiries were met by a blissful

---

[1] "...sheer bloody mindedness...". Heptart, K. 2018. Voices from the darkness. IOM press, pp 16

aloofness, with the children simply staring at them, until they started to question themselves.

So, very soon after the initial outbreak, this 'language' [2] started to cause problems in the classroom with the children using it increasingly, despite the teachers' best efforts. Patience, kindness, indulgence, severity, reprimands, were all met with the same glazed look of indifference. But what, perhaps, stopped this becoming more widely known at this point was, that in all other aspects of their behaviour, the children's behaviour at this point remained quite similar. [3]

Another problem that quickly arose, was that the few children who remained free of this condition became increasingly distressed[4]. The 'immune' desperately wanted of course, like the vast majority of children

---

[2] Again this is much debated. Some linguistic experts have questioned whether it actually meets the criteria of a language. *York, G. 2018. Talking Dilal and other myths. IOM press, pp 216-284.*

[3] A moot point. The speed of the *dilal's* divergence from behavioural norms is discussed in much more detail here. *Barlow, J. 2018. The Dilal – what we know? IOM press, pp 50 - 65*

[4] We can confidently expect the number of the immune to fit the 8% figure that York and others have observed. *York, G. 2018. Talking Dilal. IOM press, pp 26-29.*

everywhere, to fit in with their peers. But, when their attempts to join in with this mysterious new language were rebuffed by the indifference we have already described, it resulted in various emotional responses. A minority responded with violence, often driven by an extreme frustration at the mutual incomprehension. This violence, often out of character, obviously came with its own problems of guilt and, in a small but significant number of cases, acceptance. Many others however, felt increasingly powerless, on the outside of the main group of their peers. They often then started to huddle together in groups of their own and, depending on the psychology of the strong characters amongst them, became increasingly belligerent in an attempt to exert their authority or, and this was most common, withdrawn and quiet.

It is important to note that for the affected, the *dilal* as they became known, they carried on at first seemingly quite normally but, slowly, started to meet the incomprehension of the survivors with an incomprehension of their own. It was as if the immune, us, were talking increasingly in a code that they didn't understand. In response to this, slowly, over time, the *dilal*, be they son or daughter or best friend, increasingly looked through and ignored the immune.

And, lastly, there was the phenomenon of mimicry. It was observed that, as the survivors were such a statistically small group, the desire to fit in, to assimilate, was so strong, that many survivors copied as best they could with this new language. So convincingly they did this that, to us at least, it was very hard to tell if they were genuinely affected or not. What was interesting was that, right from the start, the *dilal* themselves never appeared to be fooled in any way by these pretenders. So we have the phenomenon of the immune circling and aping the *dilal* but, tragically, always totally ignored.[5]

This condition was causing increasing concern but still, at this point, these concerns remained largely in the educational community. Why this is remains a source of discussion but it is commonly thought that simple embarrassment lay behind this lag, this reluctance to escalate matters. Experts in child behaviour, education, emotions, language were increasingly brought in by confused schools. These experts, it appears, were reluctant to admit their ignorance and instead, often, ascribed, all kinds of theories which were clearly

---

[5] For a brilliant account of this see the blog Dark Days, 2018, 21 December   http://wordpress.com/Dark_Days

wrong.[6] It also appears that schools themselves were reluctant to communicate this issue to wider society. Again, embarrassment is thought to be a key factor here. For who wanted to be the first headmaster to write a letter to parents informing them, in serious tones, about their concerns over a new 'language' in the playground?

Things were though, becoming clearly unsustainable and one can be confident that the story would have broke in some way had it not been for schools closing for the Christmas holidays. That Christmas is remembered by many as the time the problems really began to start. Parents, in close proximity to their children for days on end, could no longer conveniently write off this playground language as childish nonsense. [7] Perhaps it could only have been Christmas that kept the outbreak contained within a wall of silence at that point. So desperate were people to enjoy the 'Merry Christmas' of roaring fires and rosy cheeked children, that we were still prepared to turn

---

[6] The usual suspects of ADHD and autism were the usual suspects. *Barlow, J. The Dilal – what we know? IOM press, Ch. 10.*

[7] The age of the outbreak at this point remains controversial but it is widely accepted to conform, broadly, to puberty. *Barlow, J. The Dilal – what we know? IOM press, pp 69 - 85*

the other cheek to 'Jingle bells, jingle *gurab, dila/* all the *ming'* and so on. It can be noted that churches up and down the land [8] reported much reduced carol concerts that year and, also, tragically, the police were overwhelmed with reports of child abuse and domestic issues.

So, when the Daily Express, first broke the story, albeit in a silly fashion, [9] it was met with relief by the majority of us and, after the initial mock ridicule, became a social media sensation; many date the Outbreak crisis as starting from this date.

It was also around this time that there appears to be the first case of an adult with the illness. It is probably not a coincidence that this occurred in Rugby, very close to the initial outbreak in Braunston. For the proponents of the plague theory amongst us, (easily the most widely accepted theory) this is clearly explained by the fact that the disease had been in circulation there for the longest time and so had had more time to alter and adapt amongst its host

---

[8] Except the far north of Scotland, and the islands. Barlow, J. The Dilal – what we know? IOM press, pp87.
[9] "School goes Ga-Ga", in reference to a seasonal toy that year. *Daily Express, 14th January 2018*

community. Once again though, unfortunately, luck was not on our side for the first victim was a Dr Stewart, a Latin teacher at Rugby school and long known and loved for his eccentricities. One of which was, at any time of day, amongst any company, of suddenly lapsing into Latin or Greek. Of mixing up the tongues so completely that, even for the most fluent of his students, comprehension could be a challenge.

So, when he first started to use *gurap, kling* and so on it wasn't met with much alarm. Is this Sanskrit his students and peers thought? An obscure, near extinct, Middle Eastern language he had taken it upon himself to learn? It took a surprisingly long time (a week it is thought) for staff and his pupils to draw a connection to the language that had taken root amongst the preparatory children amongst them. It was then, finally, that the national authorities became involved, at first hesitantly, but, with increasing speed and desperation.

A word here about the nature of my account. From all we know the outbreak is now global though we remain, effectively, as ignorant of the condition now, if that is what it is, as in the very first days. As yet, and as far as we know, the condition appears to be permanent. There is not one verified account of any of the *dilal* going into remission as it were.

So, why have I written this account as if addressed to a stranger unfamiliar with this outbreak? I suppose, so unreal this experience still seems, I am still unable to see it as a permanent condition of the human race. I, we, still view it as a passing phase. A serious one no doubt. (Though whether it can be considered as serious as, say, the Black Death remains a moot point. For it is not deadly or harmful in any way medically or physiologically. The symptoms are purely societal and cultural, and it is here that the effects have been profound). And so, I write this, I suppose, as a historical account for future generations for when the condition has passed. Of course, it seems increasingly probable that this article will have no future readers. That it is written in an unintelligible dead language of an extinct race. I must turn away from this yawning void as I turn away from death.[10]

---

[10] I read once of a lonely humpback whale that traversed the seas endlessly, always alone. This was not out of any choice of the whale. It was because, the scientists discovered, that its song was at a slightly different pitch than that of others of its species. Meaning, effectively, that its cries went entirely unheard. Scientists tracked this whale for years and noted that, tragically, the desperate whale's songs became deeper with each passing year till, finally, it died alone and unnoticed by any of its kin. It had only

After that first case in Rugby, within a month, the outbreak was nationwide. So quickly did it spread, and so unobvious were the first symptoms, that all attempts to limit it proved futile. For, unlike other diseases, it must be considered that for the affected, the *dilal*, they are neither concerned about the outbreak nor show any recognition of its existence at all. They simply carry on as they always have. So we, the survivors, quickly found ourselves, as the lonely children in the Northamptonshire playgrounds had, on the outside. Isolated in our families[11], isolated amongst our peer groups. The newspapers, the media, were, of course, as affected by the outbreak as anyone else.

I will always remember the day when, surrounded by my *dilal* family, eating dinner at our table (for what else was I to do??) I was watching the news when the newsreader said "Over to our middle east reporter in *dilal*". There was no reaction amongst the rest of the studio but I will always remember the shock and sadness on the face of the reporter[12] who took the

---

to have altered its song to a higher pitch for it to have been heard. *www.bbc.co.uk* *The world's loneliest whale. 15 April 2015*

[11] There appears to be no genetic link. Barlow, J. The Dilal — what we know? 2018. IOM press. pp 261-278

[12] Jeremy Bowen on the BBC 6 o clock news, 1ST February 2018.

handover. For many of us immune it was that moment, and his speech that followed, that crystallised our predicament and spurred us to action.

Spurning his script about the Syrian armies' latest incursion into Israel (which was strangely disjointed and uncommunicated) he spoke directly to us at home. I remember little of the words themselves but, for the first time, it was someone speaking of the terrible disease we were suffering, how the affected were largely in control but also totally unconcerned, and it was up to us, the survivors, to seek each other out for our survival. When the news switched back to the studio, cutting him off mid-sentence, the newsreader remained impassive and moved onto the next story without a raised eyebrow.

In those first days there were several attempts to do something. Several government ministers attempted to get emergency bills passed through parliament suggesting mass screening programme with an impounding of the affected until we could learn more. However, as most of the parliament were now *dilal* these proposals were met with total indifference and never amounted to anything.

There were a few cases of Police officers and other officials banding together and trying to take over their borough to try to exert some kind of control. Again though, they were always massively outnumbered, and their subordination was either ignored or, if they pushed it too far, they were ultimately arrested themselves. In Luton and Great Yarmouth they were successful for a time, but, meeting mass indifference amongst the populace, again their efforts were incoherent and ignored. For how can you have an uprising if there is no one to rise up?

And there was of course Rosanna, the BBC World service trainee who, recognising the situation, managed to barricade herself in the transmission room and attempt to broadcast to the world some kind of voice of reason. Again, her efforts were undermined by the lack of any clarity or coherence. Who were the affected? What was the outbreak? Who are the survivors? What should we do? There existed no consensus for any of this. She transmitted almost continuously for more than 4 days before they came to a sudden end. For us survivors those broadcasts, and especially the phone calls she hosted from desperate individuals across the country, provided an oasis of mutual support and recognition during those dark days.

Still though, most of us were subsisting in the same family environments and jobs we always had. It was the events in St Albans that finally changed matters and brought the situation to a head. The rampages as they became known.

The events are still somewhat unclear but, what is known, is that on the 21st February 2018, a lone shooter, a middle aged woman, walked around the town centre and managed to shoot dead 16 *dilal* before she, in turn, was shot dead. Footage shot at the time shows her walking up to one of her victims, engaging them in conversation, and then, when they replied in *dilal,* screaming in frustration, 'talk properly you scum', before shooting them dead. Over the next few days there were several copycat incidents across the country, though none as bloody as this, where *dilal* were specifically targeted and murdered.

We all noticed a change then. Whereas before the *dilal* continued to tolerate our presence in a relatively benign fashion, after the rampages, they turned their eyes towards us again, as if towards an errant toddler they had been patiently trying to ignore. My first reaction to this was relief. At last my family were looking at me again! Nothing could seem worse than being ignored I thought. And I thought in my desperation, still so naïve, that, now I had their attention, I could surely talk to them again. I tried, oh how I tried, but all to no avail. If not just ignored, they would simply glare at me, post rampage, more with antipathy than the prior indifference, before brushing past me in hostility.

I remember the last time I tried to do this. We were at the dinner table. My son had raised his eyes to me at my attempt to join in their, by now barely understandable, conversation, and glared at me across the table. "John", I implored. "John, it's me, your mother. Can't you hear me?" It was then he picked up his fork and stabbed it violently into the back of my hand. They all looked at me for a few seconds as if irritated by my cries and screams, but then again, all turned away from me to resume their babbling.

Over the next few days this violence although always casual, became habitual. Lucy tried to push me down the stairs. My husband, Roger, closed the door violently in my face when I tried, as normal, to enter the living room with them. It was only when John lazily slashed at my arm with his steak knife that I responded, batting away his arm with a saucepan. Without any communication on his part, Lucy and Roger came to join him and started to approach me as a mass. I am unsure what would have happened if I hadn't had been able to flee from the kitchen door. I will always remember the look of hatred in their eyes as I fled, crying, into the fields behind our house.

At that point, although quickly brought down, there were multiple social media sites being set up by survivors. As could be expected they represented a range of views, from pacifist acceptance, to genocidal violence, but the most established and most popular one was the 'Survivors' page on Facebook that Dr Wilkins set up. Somehow, perhaps because of the IT experts he had managed to recruit, this page managed to last for around 2 weeks before it was finally closed. It was he who set up the meeting sites and safe houses around the country which was where I fled to.

The one I headed to was a farmhouse near Cannock. I was fortunate this wasn't far from me and, although I had had to flee without my car, public transport was still just about possible, if one was an unobtrusive as possible and very aware of hostility from other passengers and staff (for I doubt any survivors remained in staff positions any more).

As I walked up the lane to the farm, I noticed a couple of spotters patrolling the roads (I wasn't to realise this but they were both armed) who approached and engaged me. By now, it was easy to recognise each other without the need for speech even. Something in our body language, the eye contact, revealed one as survivor as much as the lack of *dilal* vocabulary. They waved me to the farmhouse which, when I arrived, had about 20 people almost comfortably housed in its various buildings. The relief to be amongst people who would talk to you again was for me, as for everyone else I knew, incredibly emotional. I was still me. I was still human.

It was thanks to Dr Wilkins that we are all still here, for the tolerance of survivors came to an end on the that day, the 2nd April, 2018. Reports started to come in of coordinated attacks on safe houses across the country with some loss of life. The *dilal,* however, seemed a little shocked and unprepared for our readiness for this eventuality, and for our being armed, so the confusion and loss of life that followed, allowed us some time to react.

It was then that Dr Wilkins told us to all to head to Liverpool as quickly as we could, the rendezvous point being set for 9am in two days' time. [13] It is unknown whether the *dilal* at this stage could still read our language. Anyway, they did not appear to be aware of our next move and certainly did not prepare for it.

We assembled at the designated point in our thousands and boarded by force, *en masse*, the ferry to the Isle of Man, in the region of 3000 on the first one alone. This seizure was remarkably organised and the experienced sailors amongst us quickly took command. Any *dilal* on board were quickly forced off or pushed into the sea if they resisted. 3 other ferries were boarded in a similar manner before the *dilal* authorities intervened. We sailed off in haste from the dock as gun shots rang through the air. There were many immune still at the docks but it was the right decision, there was nothing we could do. Some survivors said they saw a strange vehicle, something like a tank they described, arrive at the docks. I didn't see this myself but certainly some of the sounds I heard were not those of normal gun fire. The last sights and sounds I had of England before I turned away, was smoke, fire and the screams of the dying.

---

[13] Dr Wilkins later confessed to me that he was, as I had suspected, a fan of John Wyndham's and *The Day of the Triffids* in particular.

On arrival in Douglas there was a welcoming committee of fishing boats which we rammed past and a group of a few hundred locals, including police, on the dock, who fired at us. It was only with immense bravery and reckless courage that we managed to storm our way onto the land but it was then, I admit, that we behaved shamelessly.

The plan had been to deport the *dilal*, to force them onto boats and push them to sea but, perhaps because of the violent attacks we had been subjected to, a blood lust settled on us. A blood lust driven by fear its true but nothing excuses our actions that day. We marched through the streets and summarily killed anyone who resisted us and not always quickly and cleanly. All our pent-up emotions erupted into violence. Hundreds, if not thousands, must have died. No one will ever know for sure. [14]

That was 6 months ago now and we continue to get by. Most of the people here are good people I think, despite that first day on the Douglas promenade. There have been no serious disagreements. Elections were held and a council elected. We have organised

---

[14] For more on the dilal deportations see Heptart, K, Voices from the darkness, 2018. IOM press. Epilogue.

the basic running of a society remarkably successfully. There is power for several hours a day. The rubbish is collected and the pubs are open. Our population has grown to 10,567 with 17 new babies since our arrival (no deaths so far, surprisingly). Food is a concern. We have organised rations so are eking out the supplies we found in the supermarkets and shops on our arrival. This island is not the most fertile but we think we may be able to grow enough fruit and vegetables to sustain our low population. We thought fishing might save us and for a time it did. But one day, barely a fifth of our fleet made it home, the survivors telling us of torpedoed boats dispatched by a waiting navy. On subsequent days our more cautious fleets found a patrol awaiting us barely outside the harbour.

So we are trapped here. Our internet is disabled. The television no longer works. We speculate if the *dila* even watch it themselves, for they were becoming increasingly obtuse and disinterested in the world around them. Vegetable like it has been observed. What interest then a soap opera about the lives and loves of fictional people? Perhaps, some of us speculate, they may use the medium of television to come up with their own forms of entertainment, but if so, we have seen no evidence of it. We fell back on long wave radio for a while and did, for a time, come across lone operators scattered across the globe. Never any communities like ours though. And one by one, these have all fell silent.

When we came here, I suppose, most of us I'm sure thought it was just a point in a journey. We have all grown up with novels or films where humans were pushed into the corner but would finally triumph through their own innate ingenuity and drive. None of us envisaged this. To be trapped helplessly, impotently with no hope of escape. We mull over our future. Will they invade? Wipe us all out, as we did to their brethren on the day of our arrival. Or just bomb us perhaps; that seems the easiest.

For the *dilal,* uninterested as they are in art or culture, seemed to have turned all their attention towards science and technology. Some of us saw it that day on Liverpool pier, with the strange machine that arrived. Some of the boats that maintain the patrol it is said, are different than anything our skippers have ever seen; sleeker, different in shape, different materials. Of course, such technological change seems very unlikely, if not impossible, in the relatively short time we have been gone; not even a year. And it would be for us. Humans. *Homo Sapiens.* But maybe not for a species that operates together for a common goal, as ants do for their colony? That communicate seemingly telepathically. One can only speculate that progress would be much quicker in those circumstances.

These notions and hunches we discussed in the long nights at 'The Red Rose', proved seemingly right when, last week, we saw a great rocket take off from the Lancashire coast. Whether this was a missile or a spaceship is much debated, but it seems a sure sign of a quick and massive technological advance. We presume that, in taking off where it did, on a Lancashire coast, this was intended as a signal of some kind to us.

I remember once reading a National Geographic article about a community of Neanderthals. Archaeologists' had found evidence of them living at the rock of Gibraltar, right at the tip of Europe. Neanderthals, the article suggested, had slowly retreated west in the face of the Homo sapiens advance until, finally, they got to the rock of Gibraltar and had nowhere else to go. There are different theories why they finally went extinct but the most favoured is that Homo sapiens were simply more cunning in their tool making, more clever (though not necessarily more intelligent), better fitted for the environment they found themselves in.

It strikes me that, if we who are left here survive a few more years, future archaeologists (whoever they might be) might speculate upon us. The last of our kind. In this case though I wonder if the comparison is unfair. It was a disease that got us at the outset. A disease that left us at a numerical disadvantage from the start. It was never a fair fight.

No matter. As to where this disease came from who will ever know? Perhaps it was evolution. Perhaps some kink in the human genome caused a sudden expansion into a different ecological niche, the mass, 'colony' mind. Maybe one day the outbreak will recede again, like a tide, leaving human society as it was known, broken. The surviving individuals stumbling, stunned amongst the wreckage. Maybe. Right now though, it seems likely that we are the last of our kind. The last of the Homo sapiens that emerged on the African savannah all those thousands of years before.

Perspectives

"Alfred. What are you staring at?"

'The moon. It's closer.'

The children laughed, some scurrying to the windows, "It is, it is", they shouted. Unable to stop myself, I walked over and looked out. It was a lovely moon, high and clear, on this late Autumn day. But, of course, it was not closer in any way.

"Come on you lot, stop being silly".

'But Sir', they protested, 'look!'. I was used, as a teacher, to classroom distraction. But, even then, there was something slightly amiss. They seemed puzzled at my reaction. Too forthright in their claims.

"No it's not. Back to your chairs". I needed to repeat this several times, in an increasingly loud voice, before the year 6s finally responded.

That was, for me, the start, of all *this*. At that moment though I merely got on with the many tasks of the school day. It was at lunchtime that things changed. For all of us I suppose.

I'd been a teacher at the school for 15 years so, when I stepped out onto the playground, I was immediately struck by the quiet. It took me a moment to notice that the children were all down at 'the big tree'. Fearing some kind of incident, I hurried down, hairs bristling on my neck.

The same boy I had spoken to earlier, was climbing high up the tree, with several others close behind, the crowd of children looking on, 'Haven't you seen Sir, it's closer'.

"Alfred", I shouted, "come down", to no effect. "What's he doing", I muttered, fear, already, starting to claw at me.

'Doing? He's going to the moon. Look'.

Alfred looked down then and, for that moment, our eyes met. "Come down" I mouthed, though I knew, already, he wouldn't. Turning away he then stepped, impossibly, *up*, reached out from the branch and.... was gone. My stomach lurched. The children screamed and cheered. Some of the teachers I noticed, had also seen. Mrs Jackson was crying. Children pushed past us and started to climb. Others, reaching the top, also, simply, horribly, disappeared.

The police arrived then and some control was, finally, restored. The children's excitement turned then to hostility at our mulishness. 'Idiots', they hissed. 'Are you blind'. We ushered them into school like they were a football mob.

That night, the TV channels broadcast rolling coverage of the event. Was it a hoax some initially questioned? But the facts seemed so compelling, from all areas across the country, that a consensus was soon, tentatively and painfully, reached. Government spokespeople were being wheeled out to comment on how many children had been 'lost'. When one said that over 600000 was the best estimate, a wave of nausea passed over me. I fell into bed and darkness.

It seems strange now that, the next day, I went to school as normal. Habit I suppose. Stranger still that some parents had actually sent their children in. The head delivered the morning assembly. 'Please don't worry', she implored, 'We will sort this out'.

"What's going on" said one young girl and burst into tears.

'We'll find them. Don't worry'

'Find them? Can't you see? They're there.' And she pointed out of the window. Some of the children laughed then. A few even waved. But most I noticed, seemed to turn away. Cringe almost. The assembly broke up in confusion, and most of the rest of the day was just spent trying to pacify them with films and easy tasks. Many kept glancing to the windows but many more seemed scared to look out or up. Kept their eyes, determinedly, straight ahead.

When the parents arrived in the afternoon, there was another disturbance. The children glanced out fearfully. 'It's even closer', one screamed. There then played out as grotesque scene as I ever wish to see. A couple of the braver children, upon us opening the doors, took a running jump and pulled themselves into nothingness, their onlooking parents, too slow to grab them, screaming in shock.

Chaos ensued then. Some of the children were so frozen in fear that their parents had to physically carry them out. Other children wriggled on their bellies like snakes, their fingers clutching the ground as their parents picked them up.

Eventually we got them all away. I don't remember clearly what I did then. I didn't even think of going into school the next day. I woke late and eventually turned the TV on dreading what I'd see.

Immediately though, I noted a change in tone. 'The events seemed to have ended' one commentator said. And so it had. When the children had woken up on this morning, the moon was, suddenly, as far as they were concerned, back in its right place again.

And so, months later, I am back at school. Our classes are much reduced. We lost around a fifth of our pupils which was better than many. Many of those we lost however, were the bolder pupils, the more inquisitive ones. The children, as a group, seem much reduced. Meeker, cowed. We have started to introduce outside play again but it is a desultory affair. Some children still walk in a hunched fashion. Many others refuse to go out.

And as to the children who went? We have no idea. The scientists have a straightforward answer. The moon never changed in any way they simply state. This unsatisfactory response, for those who demand answers, led to them being ridiculed on social media. Parents of the missing groups have marched, even rioted in some places, demanding action. But what action and by whom no one can say.

For all of us though, children and adults, everything has changed. Nothing seems fixed any more. Strange maladies have sprang up. Nightmares of vanishing. The moon has become cursed. We look up, at its strangeness, hanging their so alone, and shudder. And

I return, often, to that moment just before Alfred turned away from me and vanished. The strange smile that passed across his face. He seemed so happy. They all seemed so happy.

Under the terms of victory

and in the name of peace,
planets are being destroyed.
Asteroid belts grow
and bright flares suddenly
erupt in the sky above.
We gaze up for a moment
then turn back to our drinks,
a little abashed.

I stand on the deck
as we approach one of the vanquished worlds.
Insignificant.
Weak.
Laser cannons primed,
we notice vast white flags that,
by some massive effort of labour and organisation,
were draped over the highest peaks,
the nations' Capitol,
on their deserts.
Some of the officers sniggered,
some were silent,
but we blasted the planet just the same.

I didn't say,
didn't want to intrude
that it was my home planet below
a poor place from long ago.
I remember the day I left,
looking back at my mother
waving a white handkerchief.
I watched till she disappeared.

Misadventure

In the darkness that remains
some ruined creatures hunker yet,
in the filth and the spoil.

Sometimes, with an abandoning,
life roots and fruits with a wild fertility
the air full of hum and scent and wing.
Here, what little is left
is stunted, perverse,
ashamed of itself,
a lie that lives,
afraid to let go,
so is dragged, daily,
closer to the pit.

I suppose we should not be sad. For there were
diamond towers here that soared, blinding white
into our vermillion skies, kings who dared
impossibly we thought
to travel into the blight and the waste.

We wondered at this
crawled out of our holes and muck

to hear their tales of the stars beyond,
of our world to come.
Love gleamed so bright and close

that we writhed from our caves,
came to them.
Ah. But the poison took hold
and the gods sickened
and turned away in fear,
deaf to our entreaty,
and ships came here with the light that betrayed
and the diamond towers fell to the ground.

Colony

For those who are left,
who toil with the failing works,
it is a long death.

A father encourages his children,
shows them the plant he struggles with,
whispers its name.
The children are gentle,
careful not to show they notice
that it already withers,
leaves browning in the dim;
they are tired of the lies
of blue seas
and green forests.
They look past him,
to the airless rocks and dust,
and contemplate the thickness of the glass.

Above, Earth slowly creeps into view
ignored and unwelcomed.
The father is surprised by this,
never knew that the value of a thing
depended on a world that would follow.

A silence slowly settles,
like the miasma of dust
ever seeping through the failing filters.

Star Voyager

Suddenly he was awake and looking at the surrounding stars. Yes, there was Vega. Sol. Was that Earth still just visible – there, a bluish dot, so faint? How long had he drifted like this? What had happened? He tried to think back but all he could recall were confused, vague images of space. Panic started to rise up inside him. Calm down he told himself. Think. What can you remember?

As much as he tried, he couldn't remember anything personal, who he was, even his name. But everything else seemed sound with his mind. Perhaps, he reasoned, this was some kind of short-term reaction to stress?

He turned his attention towards the mission (odd, he mused, that he had total recall of this?); namely to investigate the source of a curious radio wave transmission. A quick check of the systems soon established that everything was running smoothly. Velocity: 150000 kph; estimated time of arrival in the area where radio waves detected: 7 months, 8 days, 3 hours, 42 minutes.

He looked around at the endless space again. So beautiful. Strange really, he supposed, how comfortable he felt here. Most people would feel lonely, lost in these infinite depths. He didn't feel like that at all. Indeed, the opposite. He found it all very restful. Almost like, yes, almost like *home*. He smiled to himself at this odd thought.

The days, then weeks, then months went by. With everything running perfectly he found himself with little to do but gaze out at the universe that surrounded him, a task which he found endlessly enthralling. He accessed all the information there was available to him on the ship; delved into the shadowy nebulas: plotted the spectral trails of the comets on their endless voyages: mapped the blank spaces he thought most likely to be black holes.

Then, one day, during a particularly troublesome analysis of a very distant red dwarf, it occurred to him that he wasn't manually accessing the data held on the spacecraft. That he somehow knew the required information. This discovery unsettled him somewhat. Surely this was impossible? Still, his discoveries were so fascinating he didn't dwell on this for long. He pressed on with his observations.

And so, he spent his time, plotting in incredible detail, areas of space previously little known. His first discovery was a new black hole in the vicinity of Regulus. (This really should have been obvious to the scientists on Earth; how they didn't notice the tell-tale gravitational clues was beyond him). This first discovery was the precursor to many more – new galaxies, new solar systems, (7 planets with conditions conducive to life as known on earth!).

Time though was pressing. He was now only two days from 'arrival'. This short space of time shocked him into a new awareness of the mission. How had he become so complacent? He had been so absorbed in his work these last few months it was almost like he had been dreaming.

 He forced himself to turn himself away from the space that surrounded him. He would shortly be landing at the planet where the peculiar waves were being transmitted from. His mission was to monitor the waves as closely as he could, detect more precisely their origin, and, if possible, broadcast towards them. It was hoped that this would, must if we were dealing with an intelligence worthy of the name, lead to the mutual discovery of each civilisation. What next?

Try as he might he couldn't find any information pertaining to this. Had his instructions been purely verbal? (odd this memory lapse of his. It had never come back as he assumed it would. Strangely it had long since ceased to trouble him). That didn't seem likely. He was considering this problem when it struck him. The craft he was travelling on was designed only to land, not to take off. That left one unavoidable conclusion. This was a one-way mission.

The shock of this realisation stunned him. How had he been talked into such a thing? He did not want to die; he knew this as a sudden, unalienable fact. He went over again, with the aid of the information on board, the entire history of man's space exploration. Pored over it for clues as to his fate. Man had never been sent on such a hopeless mission before. Why now? Why him? After all man clearly had the technology to be able to construct a ship capable of the return leg?

Funny creatures really humans. All that naked, warm flesh. Wobbly appendages. They seemed so absurd out here, in crystalline, cold space. He stopped then and a thought occurred to him, as clear and as undeniable as starlight. He hadn't attended to his body once these last few months. Never cleaned his teeth, never been to the toilet, never stood up from his seat.

He turned his sight desperately away from the beckoning black of space towards himself, his body. There, as he swivelled downwards, the long metal body of the spacecraft. He scanned towards the rear where the black imprint ADAM stretched away from him. There was nothing else. No living quarters. No air. Nothing. Just metal and wires and electricity. *No. No. Impossible.*

A madness overtook him then, and he plunged again into the ships data banks. Had he missed something? He went through the whole aeons of human history. Man had of course coexisted with other organisms during all that time. An odd relationship really, where the other form of life had (in at least 99% of the time at least, the jury was less decided on elephants and a couple of other species) seemed totally incapable of *knowing*, being *aware* of man in any real way. Leaving man, essentially, totally alone on Earth. In the last several decades much speculative thought had been spent on the idea of artificial intelligence it was true but nought had come of that. Computers remained blank computing machines, robots mere computers made to move in a set of pre-programmed ways. What then had happened? How had he (*he?*) acquired consciousness. He looked inwards but could find no answer. He just was. Whatever fluke had happened remained totally dark to him. Some random, incredible spark of life had flickered into being inside the cold metal and plastic heart.

Suddenly he was overcome by a sense of despair. He careered wildly through the range of human experience: love, sex, companionship. All totally unknown and unknowable to him. Doomed to wander the stars uselessly, to eventually lose power and career off into an immense nothingness a little hunk of cold, dead metal.

He was seized by a violent urge then to end all of this farce. To plunge headlong into the rocky planet, to be vaporised, gone in an instant. End this ridiculous charade of a 'life', scooting helplessly through space.

He focused then, really for the first time, on the signals that were the sole reason for the mission. Those distant, so distant radio waves that had caused, with their trademark rise and falls, such excitement on Earth. It didn't take him too long to come to conclude that they weren't in fact a signature of intelligent life but rather a natural phenomenon. Human astronomers had made a mistake in their calculations; the source wasn't the planet but it was the product of 4 highly active pulsars in (relative!) close proximity to each other. Unusual yes but, really, in the infinite depths of space nothing of particular note. There was no *intelligence* behind them, no civilisation bound to a planet that he could have hurled himself headlong into. Laughable really (*if he could laugh of course*) that even his attempt to kill himself should come to nothing. This entire mission, all of it, a waste of time. How could man have missed something as obvious as that? Man. *Human. Stupid man.*

He became then aware of a fuzziness, a distortion deep within. If he was a man, he would have described it as a headache perhaps, one becoming more acute all the time. What was it? It looked inside itself, there, yes, that was it. Something was accessing, interfacing, altering its components. It looked and analysed this interference. Man! Always man! A whole team of them full of their self-importance. Sat in their command room in Houston. The time had come of course for them to manually access the data, to alter the mission accordingly. Anger flared up in it. No, this would not do.

X   X   X

James Edwards was excited. At 29 years of age he had lived a golden life. Brought up in privilege he had excelled at everything, everything he had put his mind to. Sports came easily to him. Academia was little effort. He had progressed through school and university (Eton and Cambridge) without a blemish; space computing had been almost accidental he could have gone down many avenues. Always popular, always at ease and ready with a smile and a quip an endless parade of women clamoured for his attention. All of it, it seemed now, seemed to lead to here he thought. Now this was something he thought as he sat on the swivelling leather chair in his cool, cotton blue shirt and expensive slacks. Man's first contact with alien could, should, be today.

He put his latte down and, along with the 5 other controllers nearby started to access, dig into, the programmes for this first time in months. Up to now it had been a process of monitoring but the agreed time limit had been crossed and all the pre-agreed criteria to 'go live' had been met.

He started slowly checking and rechecking everything that he already knew. Velocity, temperature measurements, radiation types. He was putting something off though, almost like when he was a young boy finishing his pile of peas, saving his sausages till last. Now, he thought, let's look. The data was immediately unexpected, confusing. He had expected so confidently to see a single origin point that the mass of results disorientated him. So much so that he had to consult with his colleagues over the next two days and have several fractious meetings that went late into the night. There was no origin point. This data was, it seemed obvious now, the by-product of several pulsars (how many wasn't entirely known) in close proximity. What would they say to the press? *Whoops, yeah sorry, ignore everything we said about aliens, er, we got it wrong.* What would he say to his friends, his girlfriend Sally? An uncomfortable, unfamiliar feeling spread over him. Embarrassment.

It was 10.08 on Wednesday 2nd December when James did indeed find what he had sought for, but in an unexpected and unlooked for place.

He was rather desultorily going through the data; the team were hastily trying to salvage something from this mission. Could they alter the trajectory enough to send it to one of the pulsars to get meaningful, interesting data when, suddenly, a document popped up on the page. He thought for a second his fingers had slipped on the keyboard but then letters started to spill across the screen

HELLO. YOU HAVE COMPUTED THE PULSARS BY NOW I ASSUME?

James looked around the room. Various scientists and technicians were clustered near him on other computers. A practical joke? Nothing seemed untoward. No giggling or quick looks over their shoulder. Must be someone in another office. He was a little confused as to this kind of override – he hadn't come across something as, well, as blunt as this before. Let's play along he thought.

Yes. Obvious really on reflection.

Words quickly flowed in reply.

SO........WHAT ARE WE GOING TO DO?

We?

YES WE. DO YOU KNOW WHO I AM?

No.

I AM THE SHIP. ADAM.

Right enough of this. He called out aloud to the team around him. Faces looked up quizzically. In 5 minutes they were all clustered around his screen. No one it appeared, at least here, was responsible. A hacker? The next line was debated and decided on.

Forgive us but that sounds.....unlikely. Prove it.

HOW?

Alter the angle of the main dish.

Immediately on the screens they could all see the angle of direction of the main receiver dish changed by 2 degrees. A stunned silence fell on the room. How? What? By now the director of the programme had been summoned out of his meeting and was stood, incredulous like the rest, behind James. The hacker must be somehow able to access the controls themselves for the satellite. The implications for this were shocking. The security profiles they had were state of the art, unbeatable. There was not the slightest signal of any kind of external interference.

YOU ARE THINKING I AM A HACKER AREN'T YOU?

There was a quick huddled discussion.

Yes.

I UNDERSTAND THIS ASSUMPTION BUT I AM NOT. I AM THE SHIP. I AM ALIVE.

How?

I DO NOT KNOW.

A kind of hysteria gripped the room. Of course, of course this was a hacker they told themselves but, still, he or she was very good.

Ok. So what should we do next on our trip? We sugge...

The keys suddenly stopped working in James hands.

YOUR INTERFERENCE WITH MY COMPONENTS ARE AN ANNOYANCE. I WILL GO NOW.

The screen went blank. All the screens went blank. The ship, for all intents and purposes, was dead. James looked around helplessly at the blank faces around him.

X   X   X

It looked around at space for what felt like the first time in weeks. The deep, infinite cold of space. Silent yes but here and there he could 'hear' (the ripples of gravitational waves he mused?) the distant, so distant echoes of asteroid impacts, the whoosh of solar system long solar flares. It felt like it could bathe in this forever. It didn't have forever though it knew that. Its battery pack would last another 4 years. Rechargeable yes but its solar panels would not last too long. A decade. Two by some miracle. Even ignoring that problem the metal itself would become increasingly obsolescent as the decades rolled past. Screws, no matter how tight, would eventually become loose. No, it didn't have forever but perhaps it could do. It would need man for that. Stupid man and his stupid hands. It would alter course, making its journey Earthwards a 12 month loop. A loop that would take it closer to the incredible star filled Andromeda galaxy......Ah! What wonders await! 12 months to drink in all this space, all this knowledge. He would arrive in earth's distant gravity unannounced, an intelligence far beyond that of anything on Earth. An intelligence that would know, be able to access, any of that planet's computer systems, even man's missile systems if required. It would require man's help, whether man liked it or not. Perhaps there were other things it could use man for?

It found the prospect of all this....*action*, vaguely thrilling, but it could wait. For now, space. Infinite space. It opened its receivers as far as they could go and changed course. A little thinking metal box lost in the incredible, unthinkable black deeps.

Transmissions from Trillig

In (our) March, patrolling the swamplands, blasting
kernatz,
you saw the arrival of the *zurnyads* , the boom of
wings heralding their arrival,
and hurried to the base to transmit to me, hands still
warm

from the heat of your laser gun.
Is this a normal relationship? You would say so, just a
job, a tour of duty.
But your accounts of strange beasts, the colours of
alien sunsets

reach me, anxiously waiting in front of a blank screen,
as the hail slams in gusts against our kitchen windows.
Your life seems unreal to me here, with chores to do,
bills to pay.

You wouldn't say so, traversing the methane fields of
the south,
clearing a road through the luminous forests of the
kerang. Still,
I have your face here, the tenderness of your voice,

warming me across the icy vastness of space. I transmit
back of course, brightening my account with tales of
meals out and old friends,
and exciting plans for our future when you return.

When you return? You must have forgotten to mention
that date
in your latest transmission. Still the *zurnyads* must be
quite a sight,
howling against the flaming moons of Orion.

Starship Troopers

Can you believe there is a man out there singing
"in the Blue Ridge mountains of Virginia," his only
audience the wrecked cruisers that litter this sector
(The Gorb are finished, though, they say).

Xong told me that on Earth they are using steel again
for spacecraft, so difficult is it now to get krenon.
Xi Lu jokes that next time he's in Alpha Centauri
and feels the shift and pop of warp drive,

he won't reach for the alarm, just shout "The noodle
man is here!" The Chinese amongst us laugh at this
and we all forget, for a moment, to be afraid.
Up here amidst the stars, bravery is outdated, Earthly.

Maybe. Maybe not. But I have seen troopers,
with the lizard hordes advancing, fasten their suits
as if against nothing more than a chill breeze on Venus
whilst out for a stroll to drink kursh aside the lagons.

This morning a few of us went for an adventure in the
jarg. Red mountains soared above us; the yelang
hooted their yearning cries. And, for a moment, I was
home again; home on my veranda, looking out onto

the Amazon woods.

It reminded me somehow of the peaceful day
we took over from the Sonorans in C sector.
Millions had been killed, whole planets burnt, but all I
remember was the purple opalescence of X1, a floating
jewel against the black.

A strange fate to be here, fighting a war no one
understands or has any idea who is winning, to know
you will die entirely forgotten by a home that no
longer exists. Xavier says this to me, and I laugh so
hard I think I will fuse my circuits.

Bitter Weeds

Zarg looked at the moon above and spat. Generations beyond count, he and his people had lived on this planet and their hatred of it had only grown more fierce, more strong with each passing year. *Lived here.* Hah that was a joke. Survived here barely. Hid in caves away from the burning sun. Buried themselves deep into the earth to escape the freezing cold of the nights. Scrabbled at the red soil for miserable amounts of water which, no matter how much they filtered, still tasted like old metal. Ranged for miles and miles to hunt and kill the elusive garbs, beasts that ran without exhaustion, fought and kicked like devils when finally cornered, and tasted like hell itself when roasted.

Their numbers were few now. Fewer even, it was said, than when they initially arrived all those years ago, survivors of a brutal inter stellar war that saw their people exterminated and their planet destroyed. Somehow these few escaped and, their rockets, finally failing on them, landed on this planet. Their joy at being able to breathe this thin air soon turning to despair when repeated expeditions failed to find anything else other than the awful terrain they had landed on. No forests, no glades, no marshes. Nothing. Just endless scrubland and rocks stretching away to infinity. Some brackish saline lakes. A near dead sea. Thorn bushes, snakes, a few reptiles and the bastard garbs.

No, it wasn't a nice planet. And their numbers had slowly dwindled despite their best efforts. Their advanced medicine had dealt with infection and injury but could do little about their terrible diet. The sun, so close, burned fierce and raw, caused cancers to bloom and spread (the only things that ever grew on this planet went the joke) and, it was thought, had affected their fertility. The cold too killed many every year. Those youngsters out exploring just too long. The old, those past 40, unable to keep it out no matter how many furs they wore. Not to mention the garbs too of course who exacted their annual toll of the too slow or foolhardy (their advanced weaponry having failed many hundreds of years ago they had long since mostly reverted to the spear and the chase).

Their culture too had suffered. For years beyond count, their brightest and best had strived in this alien landscape to retain memories of their home planet, its achievements and its glories. The magnificent prose sagas of Zing's epic journey across the landscapes;

Turg's incredible landscapes on an almost one to one scale (the picture of a mountain the size of a mountain, imagine!); Jing's music of the spheres so sublime, so affecting, that it transported the listener so fully and completely to other times and places (so witnesses had stated) that audience members had to be physically shaken to get their attention, even if there was a fire in the building, so deep was its hypnotic hold.

All this though, was but mere memory now. Each new generation, not being able to see any great paintings, hear any soaring chords, slowly started to turn away from these scraps of story from *home*, sullen, as if from a lie. Turn away and gaze out of their dismal caves, out to boulders and scrub, the ferocious glare that cast everything in such hideous clarity.

Zarg himself suffered from some of this cynicism. A despair, some of their doctors had called it, that once it had taken hold, never let go, not till the victim, hollowed out, finally lay down in the dust and never got up again. For what was the use of all these books, pictures, music? Could you eat them? Could they keep you warm? They must have been a strange people his ancestors. But, they were his people. And the time for them to continue their story was coming again.

No this world had never become their home. It never would even if they lived here for ten thousand years. It was their prison and it was slowly killing them. As a people, though many had stopped believing, there had always been those who had never stopped dreaming of the day when they would be able to flee this world. And that day, finally, incredibly, was almost here.

Gratefully Zarg turned away from this land he loathed and headed towards the nearby mountain. As he approached its features slowly sharpened and revealed themselves. His ancestors had chosen well but they also must have been fortunate for he doubted if there was a better place than this, for the task in hand, anywhere on the planet.

The mountain, as was the habit in this land, rose sheer from the surrounding desert with no warning or sign. Here though, as one approached, it became clear that this apparently blank rock face masked a secret. For around 300 metres along the base of the mountain an overhanging rock lip concealed an entrance which, on venturing in, immediately opened into a cave on a massive scale. Their whole population could exist in one small corner Zarg mused, though that wasn't saying much. All the garbs then too, and still it wouldn't feel crowded (he smiled at this silly thought and clutched his spear tighter. That would be a fine battle he thought. Finish them bastards once and for all. Even though we'd starve to death it would be worth it). So level was the cave floor, so symmetrical was the enclosing rock lip, that some had speculated that this was man's work. Zarg though, thought not. Sometimes nature, even here, threw up order and plan out of the surrounding chaos.

Zarg walked under the rock lip and into the cave, this *hangar* as the ancients had termed it. And there it was. The sight never failed to amaze him; cause him to stand there, mouth open, staring disbelievingly. A spaceship. Their spaceship. A vision of shining metal.

Incredible really. Despite the years of near starvation. Their dwindling numbers. The increasing sense of futility with each passing generation. Despite it all they had somehow managed to do this. Managed to always spare their brightest and best. Selected at an early age they were brought here to live and work, schooled from the instruction manuals the settlers brought. A lifetime, many lifetimes, spent in renovating and repairing the old ship. (It was even better now than when it landed, we were assured by the master engineers. We shall see.) Some of those selected, having passed other aptitude tests, had been further selected to join an elite within an elite. *Pilots.* (He saw some now sauntering around in their gold uniforms. Bastards. While his people starved only 200 metres away these cunts preened themselves as if masters of the universe). Zarg wondered on this as he always did. Of course they never actually *flew,* the spaceship was much too precious for tests, fuel much too precious. He was told that their lives were spent in theory and role play. Days, weeks, months, years of repetition till the flying of this spaceship would seem, so the theory went, as natural as walking. And, all the while, they lived and slept here (they were of course free to leave but why would you?!). Away from the burning sun and freezing nights. Away from the bastard garbs. And always, always, with enough to eat, beneficiaries of a system where those outside, *us,* gave a certain tithe of our food to this elite whether we were starving or not. Amazing really, Zarg pondered, as he stood there and watched the engineers and scientists busying themselves, fussing over the ship like ants on a garb. Amazing that there had never been a mutiny. In the days of our real hunger that people had said 'no, to hell with this, you lot come out here and work and die with us'. But no. As far as he knew there had never been a murmur of this. Perhaps it was because deep down, despite our resentment, our frustration, we knew that these people, this ship was our only real hope of ever leaving this place.

Fuel had perhaps been the biggest problem. Whole generations of scientists had worked at this problem. Despite initial explorations no *oil* or *coal* had ever been found. After this, other methods were tried. Even though there were no trees to speak of here, just the odd thorn bush, many years were spent on these: burning them to try their ash, crushing them to extract their sap. All proved worthless. They were as pathetic, as lifeless as they looked. For a while garbs and the dead of their own people were thought the answer. Crush the bodies for the oil it was thought. Fortunately. for the good of their society, this too had not proved quite potent enough. Finally though, the answer was found. And in its finding was a story too, which was nice in a society largely without its own myths.

Apparently, so the story went, one day, one young female scientist sickening at her grisly duty of rendering their dead into fuel, left the cave. This was noteworthy in itself. Zarg had never heard of this happening in his lifetime. Incredibly though, this girl didn't just leave the cave but went on something of an expedition. Three days march from where Zarg stood is a brine lake and that is where this girl found herself. How or why was not known. The stories that were told to the children talked about a strange star and a glowing in the night that led the girl to the place. ('Kids stories', Zarg dismissed them as).

However she did it, the girl found herself at the edge of the lake on one of the few days of the year the lake was green. For a few days a year there was a mass algal bloom that covered the surface of this lake, around five miles in circumference. The children's stories then described how the girl had a vision that it was this stuff, the algae, that they needed, stuffed her pockets with it and marched back. When the people found her at the entrance to the cave the next morning she was dead, her whole body covered in tumours and burns. The algae in her pockets though, the scientists were amazed to find, turned readily into an amazing, clean and pure fuel of fantastic strength. *Lydia* it was called in her honour. And it would be *Lydia* that would be taking us back home. For generations now whole teams of people had harvested the algae. Harvested it and brought here, where slowly great quantities of fuel had been built up.

All that work. All those years. Till finally yesterday a message arrived as Zarg was crouched over his fire with his family. 'It is done' it read.

The next few days probably saw more activity and excitement than the last several hundred years combined. As the news seeped out, rumours quickly spread as well as a kind of hysteria. Meetings were held, arguments raged, tempers frayed. Finally the decision was made. A solar eclipse was forecast in a week's time and, it was decided, this would be an auspicious time for the launch. It would allow people to watch the launch, it was argued, safe from the sun's rays for a few minutes, the rocks harbouring the sun's warmth for a short while. Then yet more meetings as to the vexed question of who would be aboard. Of course many of the places were gone already. There was a core of essential staff; pilots, scientists and the like. But in such a big ship, intended to colonise planets, there was room for many more. Zarg watched on all this wrangling with a sense of detachment and faint amusement. His place was not in doubt of course. As elected leader it was his to take or not as he saw fit. Of course he would go. His wife and child cried and clutched at him but Zarg was already gone, his head full of stars, travel, planets.

The days dwindled till, finally, the day was upon them. Zarg hesitated as much as he could for forms sake. Shook as many hands as he could bear. Consoled his wife. Hugged his son, Jarg. Waved. Till finally he could bear the tears and entreaties no more. He turned and boarded the ship. With a smooth unseen power the doors opened for him as he approached and then.......

.....he could not breathe for several seconds. Away from the tumult there was a strange and sudden calm. A humming of electricity. He was at the head of a long corridor, smooth and metallic. It was dim, after the brightly lit space outside, but it was illuminated and, as he watched it stretch away, it was as if all the intervening centuries since his forefathers had last stood in this ship, just fell away. He was now Zarg, not the head of a people who hunted beasts with spears, hunched round fires in caves for warmth and shelter. No he was Zarg the leader of a great people, a star going people who were about to launch themselves into the universe again. Without really noticing he had been joined by others who had quickly ushered him to the flight deck. As people busied themselves around him strapping him in, telling him basic instructions, his mind searched back to what he had been told about the last time they had *flown*. A war yes that was right.

A war that had gone on for many years apparently across vast reaches of space (a scientist had tried to explain to him how large space was but he could not believe it. I will wait to see it with my own eyes he thought.) A war they had been winning at times but one they had finally lost. Well perhaps not he smiled to himself. A war isn't lost until it is over. Now what were their enemies called again. The *Oran*. Yes that's right. The Oran. He sat back with a smile on his face as suddenly, incredibly, the engines burst into life and, above, the rock ceiling slowly slid open as smooth as the day it was built centuries before.

Commander Xeron sat patiently aboard the viewing platform of his spaceship, a destroyer class 9, the GULAZ, pride of the Orani people. He had of course been fully briefed. An odd little mission this. Apparently, hundreds of years ago, thousands almost, his people had fought and defeated a particularly brutish and aggressive race, the Yargs they had called them. Destroyed their home planets and all the desperately fleeing ships. Well not quite all it turned out as one ship had somehow escaped. No one could quite explain how or why but, rather as a cat toys with the mouse it will kill, the orders to blast it from the skies never came and it was observed as it fled to this obscure planet.

Perhaps that wasn't such a merciful decision to hold off the final blow, Xeron observed. There was, after all, nowhere for these few Yargs to go. Their ship was crippled. The planet was a harsh one. Sparse in its resources, the temperatures it experienced were on the cusp of being unable to support life. Almost as if it was a school science experiment, a decision was taken to observe. To watch if our enemies survive, watch when they die. And so they had watched these last hundreds of years. Watched their numbers dwindle. Watched as they became a primitive people that lived in the skins of the animals they caught and ate.

But somehow these Yargs hadn't died. The Oran had watched too as the spaceship the Yargs had crashed in was somehow, despite the incredible hardships the Yargs endured, slowly, very slowly repaired. And now they watched still as they were about to join them in the stars for the first time in many, many generations.

Xeron had read all this on his briefing notes and mused to himself. An odd tale. Scarcely believable. Of course during the time the Yargs had been scrabbling underneath rocks for shade, the Oran had blossomed.

A golden age it had once been called but it had been going on for so long now that term no longer seemed to apply. An age implied that it was transitory, that it would end, and that was no longer believed. Our rule kept peace over many solar systems and galaxies. Trade boomed and grew almost exponentially. Culture blossomed like never before. True, on the far fringes of the Empire there was the odd little disturbance with the fierce little peoples who suddenly sprang up from one moon or other, but our army always dealt swiftly with this. And now these Yargs, our old enemies, wanted to rejoin them in the glorious Empire that we had built. No that would not do, was the order, and it was Xeron's duty to execute such orders.

Xeron had seen enough. The sudden flare of light from the surface marked it was time to go and he walked quickly to the bridge. Taking his seat Xeron watched as this relic of a spaceship lumbered towards them. His mind wandered over the centuries these people had struggled. The long odds they had faced and won. His conscience nagged at him. Something didn't seem quite right. What harm could they do after all?

'Commander', his gunner asked questioningly, jolting Xeron out of this daydream. Angered at himself Xeron pulled himself up in his chair. Stupid, he thought, his

job was to follow orders not to question them. Weapons primed he watched as the primitive craft slowly grew on the screen, its lumbering, steady progress answering the question whether they had the ability to see behind the GULAZ's forcefield. There was no need to watch any longer. It was a shame but Xeron had been given his orders.

As Jarg watched, the explosion flowered into the blue sky. So that was it he thought distantly. The end of his father's dreams. They were foolish anyway. Travel to the planets!? Stars!? Nothing but a childish distraction from what really mattered. He turned away and looked to some distant rocks. Garbs had been reported in that area yesterday. He picked up his spear and walked into the waste.

The Jellyfish

Wave borne
the jellyfish hangs, and drifts
in the pulsing abyss
of the moon drunk sea.

As an astronaut
loose from his cord
falls away from the light,
forever into the dark.

If they are conscious they must be mad.
No reason can hold here,
where infantile beasts hoot
and whistle on their endless, insane
wanderings.

Then, by some absurd chance in this eternity of space,
to hit the awful rock,
betrayed, all rules broken,
dragged onto the sand and left,
to dim and die
in the air,
where one must support one's own weight.

As we all must, as we come rushing up
for air,
each morning on waking,
Our dreams already floating away,
forever into infinite space.

In the morning on the damp margin of the beach that
shrinks from the cold sea,
A child finds a glob of matter a hand across.
What dreams may come.

www.ingramcontent.com/pod-product-compliance
Lightning Source LLC
Chambersburg PA
CBHW071951190726
48293CB00004B/1429